Shanower, Eric,
The marvelous land of
Oz. Vol. 5 /
2014.

cu   10/20/16

...ELOUS LAND OF OZ

VOL. 5

ADAPTED FROM THE NOVEL BY L. FRANK BAUM

Writer: ERIC SHANOWER

Artist: SKOTTIE YOUNG

Colorist: JEAN-FRANCOIS BEAULIEU

Letterer: JEFF ECKLEBERRY

Assistant Editor: MICHAEL HORWITZ

Editor: NATE COSBY

Collection Editor: MARK D. BEAZLEY

Assistant Editors: ALEX STARBUCK & NELSON RIBEIRO

Editor, Special Projects: JENNIFER GRÜNWALD

Senior Editor, Special Projects: JEFF YOUNGQUIST

SVP of Print & Digital Publishing Sales: DAVID GABRIEL

Production: JERRY KALINOWSKI

Book Design: ARLENE SO

Editor in Chief: AXEL ALONSO

Chief Creative Officer: JOE QUESADA

Publisher: DAN BUCKLEY

Executive Producer: ALAN FINE

MARVEL

visit us at www.abdopublishing.com

Reinforced library bound edition published in 2014 by Spotlight, a division of the ABDO Group, PO Box 398166, Minneapolis, Minnesota 55439. Spotlight produces high-quality reinforced library bound editions for schools and libraries. Published by agreement with Marvel Characters, Inc.

Printed in the United States of America, North Mankato, Minnesota.
102013
012014

This book contains at least 10% recycled materials.

Marvel.com
© 2014 Marvel

Library of Congress Cataloging-in-Publication Data

Shanower, Eric.
  The marvelous land of Oz / adapted from the novel by L. Frank Baum ; writer: Eric Shanower ; artist: Skottie Young. -- Reinforced library bound edition.
      pages cm
  "Marvel."
  Summary: When the Scarecrow, now the ruler of the Emerald City, is driven out by General Jinjur and her all-girl army, his friends--the Tin Woodman, a boy named Tip, and Jack Pumpkinhead--try to restore peace in this graphic novel adaptation of L. Frank Baum's classic tale.
  ISBN 978-1-61479-235-2 (vol. 1) -- ISBN 978-1-61479-236-9 (vol. 2) -- ISBN 978-1-61479-237-6 (vol. 3) -- ISBN 978-1-61479-238-3 (vol. 4) -- ISBN 978-1-61479-239-0 (vol. 5) -- ISBN 978-1-61479-240-6 (vol. 6) -- ISBN 978-1-61479-241-3 (vol. 7) -- ISBN 978-1-61479-242-0 (vol. 8)
  1. Graphic novels. [1. Graphic novels. 2. Fantasy.] I. Young, Skottie, illustrator. II. Baum, L. Frank (Lyman Frank), 1856-1919. Marvelous land of Oz. III. Title.
  PZ7.7.S453Mar 2014
  741.5'973--dc23
                              2013030127

All Spotlight books are reinforced library binding
and manufactured in the United States of America.

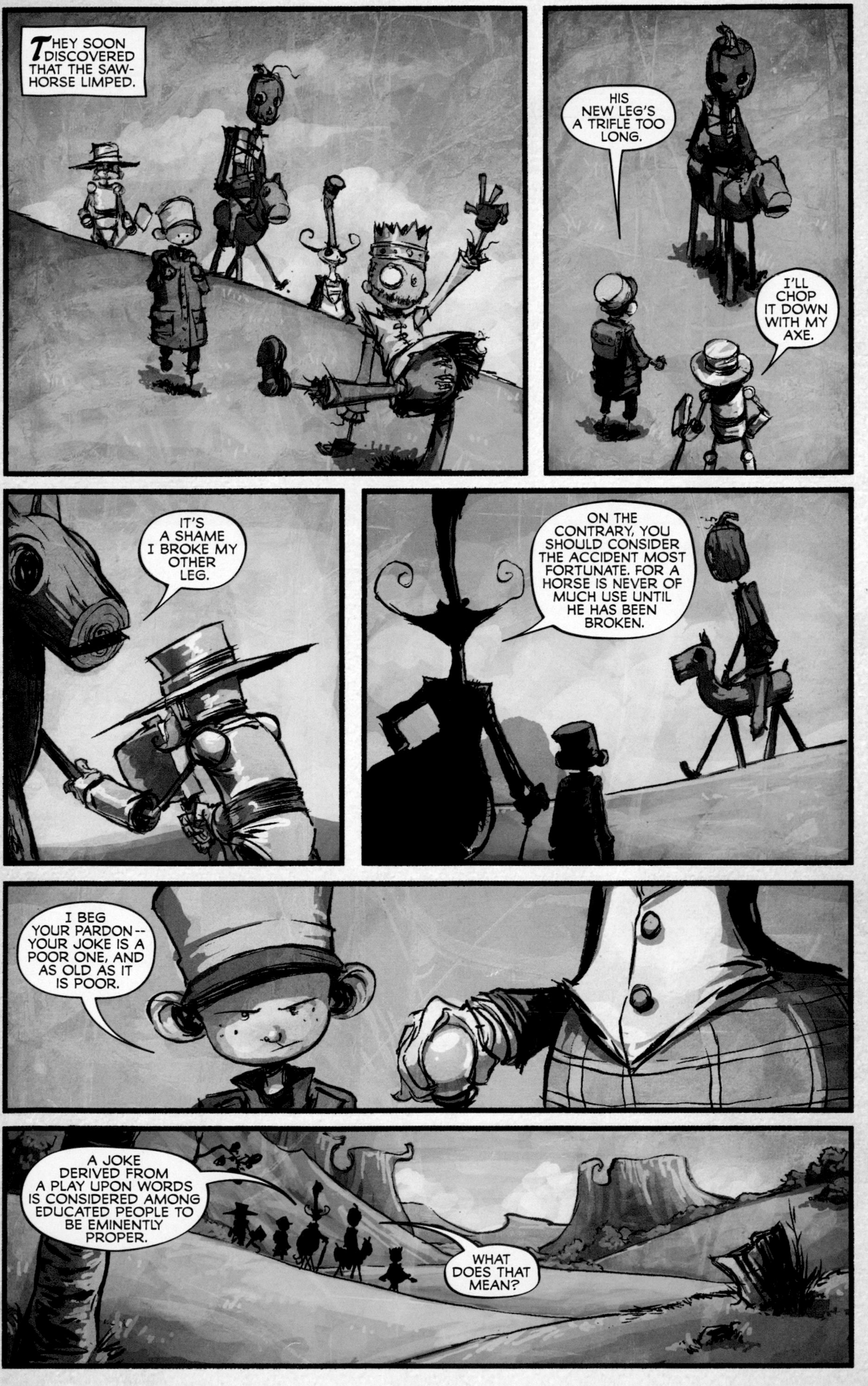
THEY SOON DISCOVERED THAT THE SAW-HORSE LIMPED.
HIS NEW LEG'S A TRIFLE TOO LONG.
I'LL CHOP IT DOWN WITH MY AXE.
IT'S A SHAME I BROKE MY OTHER LEG.
ON THE CONTRARY, YOU SHOULD CONSIDER THE ACCIDENT MOST FORTUNATE. FOR A HORSE IS NEVER OF MUCH USE UNTIL HE HAS BEEN BROKEN.
I BEG YOUR PARDON-- YOUR JOKE IS A POOR ONE, AND AS OLD AS IT IS POOR.
A JOKE DERIVED FROM A PLAY UPON WORDS IS CONSIDERED AMONG EDUCATED PEOPLE TO BE EMINENTLY PROPER.
WHAT DOES THAT MEAN?

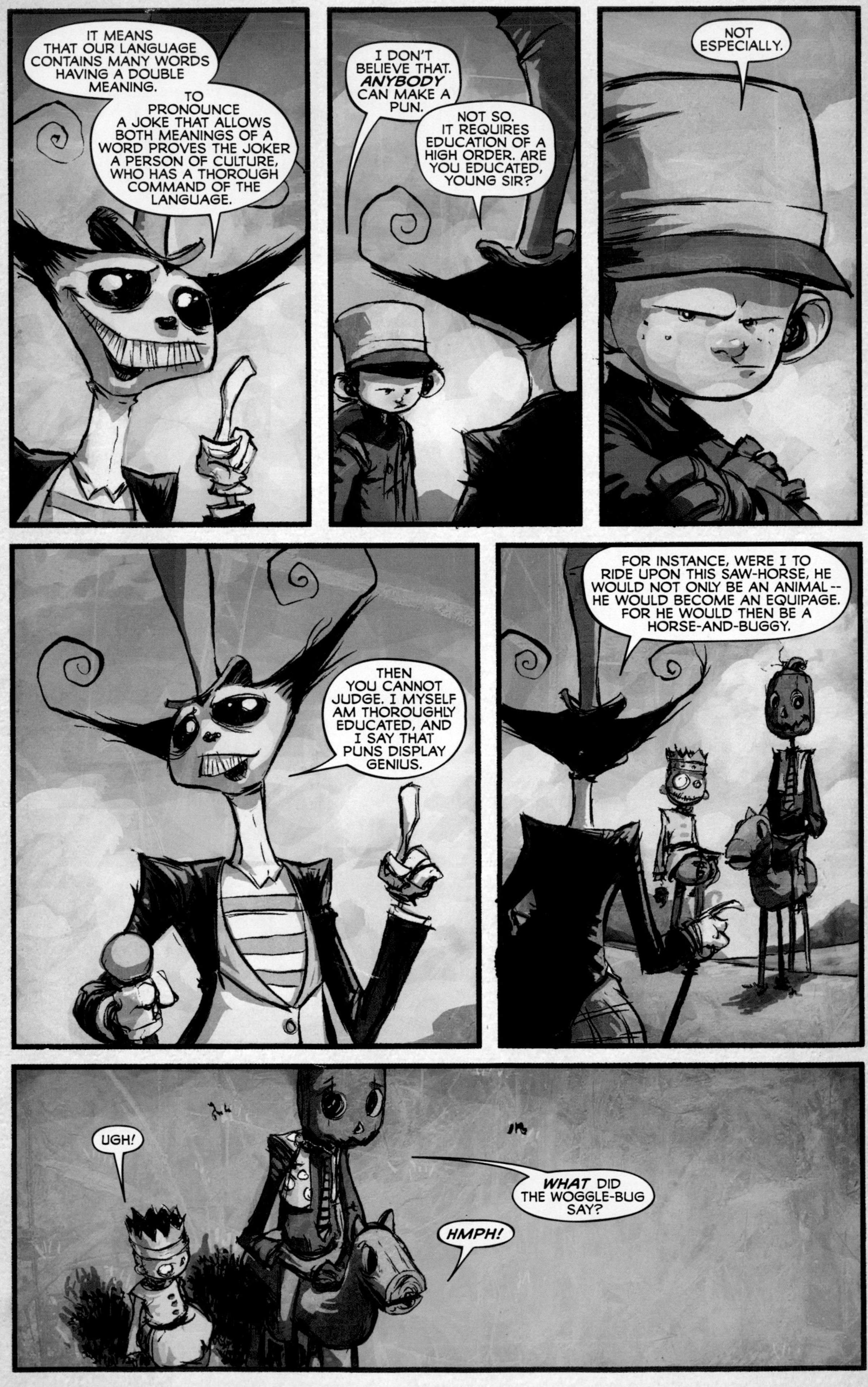
IT MEANS THAT OUR LANGUAGE CONTAINS MANY WORDS HAVING A DOUBLE MEANING.
TO PRONOUNCE A JOKE THAT ALLOWS BOTH MEANINGS OF A WORD PROVES THE JOKER A PERSON OF CULTURE, WHO HAS A THOROUGH COMMAND OF THE LANGUAGE.
I DON'T BELIEVE THAT. ANYBODY CAN MAKE A PUN.
NOT SO. IT REQUIRES EDUCATION OF A HIGH ORDER. ARE YOU EDUCATED, YOUNG SIR?
NOT ESPECIALLY.
THEN YOU CANNOT JUDGE. I MYSELF AM THOROUGHLY EDUCATED, AND I SAY THAT PUNS DISPLAY GENIUS.
FOR INSTANCE, WERE I TO RIDE UPON THIS SAW-HORSE, HE WOULD NOT ONLY BE AN ANIMAL-- HE WOULD BECOME AN EQUIPAGE. FOR HE WOULD THEN BE A HORSE-AND-BUGGY.
UGH!
WHAT DID THE WOGGLE-BUG SAY?
HMPH!

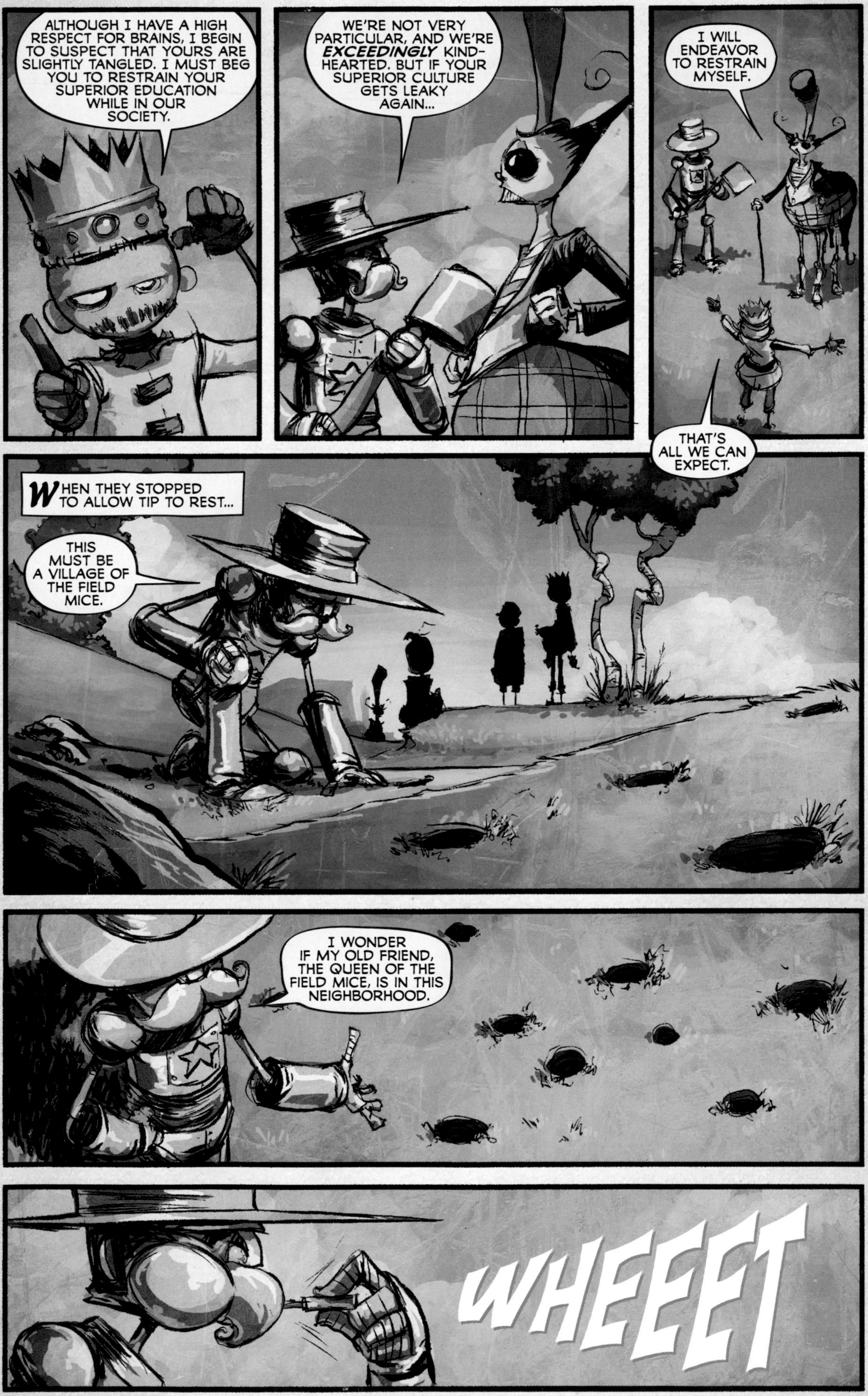
ALTHOUGH I HAVE A HIGH RESPECT FOR BRAINS, I BEGIN TO SUSPECT THAT YOURS ARE SLIGHTLY TANGLED. I MUST BEG YOU TO RESTRAIN YOUR SUPERIOR EDUCATION WHILE IN OUR SOCIETY.
WE'RE NOT VERY PARTICULAR, AND WE'RE EXCEEDINGLY KIND-HEARTED. BUT IF YOUR SUPERIOR CULTURE GETS LEAKY AGAIN...
I WILL ENDEAVOR TO RESTRAIN MYSELF.
THAT'S ALL WE CAN EXPECT.
WHEN THEY STOPPED TO ALLOW TIP TO REST...
THIS MUST BE A VILLAGE OF THE FIELD MICE.
I WONDER IF MY OLD FRIEND, THE QUEEN OF THE FIELD MICE, IS IN THIS NEIGHBORHOOD.
WHEEET

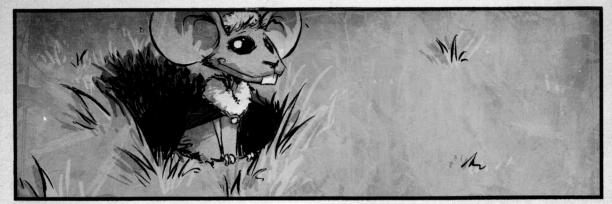

GOOD DAY, YOUR MAJESTY. I TRUST YOU'RE ENJOYING GOOD HEALTH?

THANK YOU, I'M QUITE WELL. CAN I DO ANYTHING TO ASSIST MY OLD FRIENDS?

YOU CAN, INDEED. LET ME TAKE A DOZEN OF YOUR SUBJECTS WITH ME TO THE EMERALD CITY.

WILL THEY BE INJURED IN ANY WAY?

I THINK NOT. I'LL CARRY THEM HIDDEN IN THE STRAW WHICH STUFFS MY BODY.

WHEN I UNBUTTON MY JACKET, THEY HAVE ONLY TO RUSH OUT AND SCAMPER HOME.

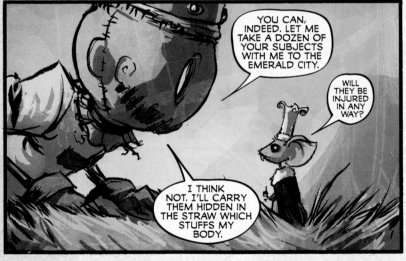

BY DOING THIS THEY'LL ASSIST ME TO REGAIN MY THRONE, WHICH THE ARMY OF REVOLT HAS TAKEN FROM ME.

IN THAT CASE, WHENEVER YOU'RE READY, I'LL CALL TWELVE OF MY MOST INTELLIGENT SUBJECTS.

I'M READY NOW.

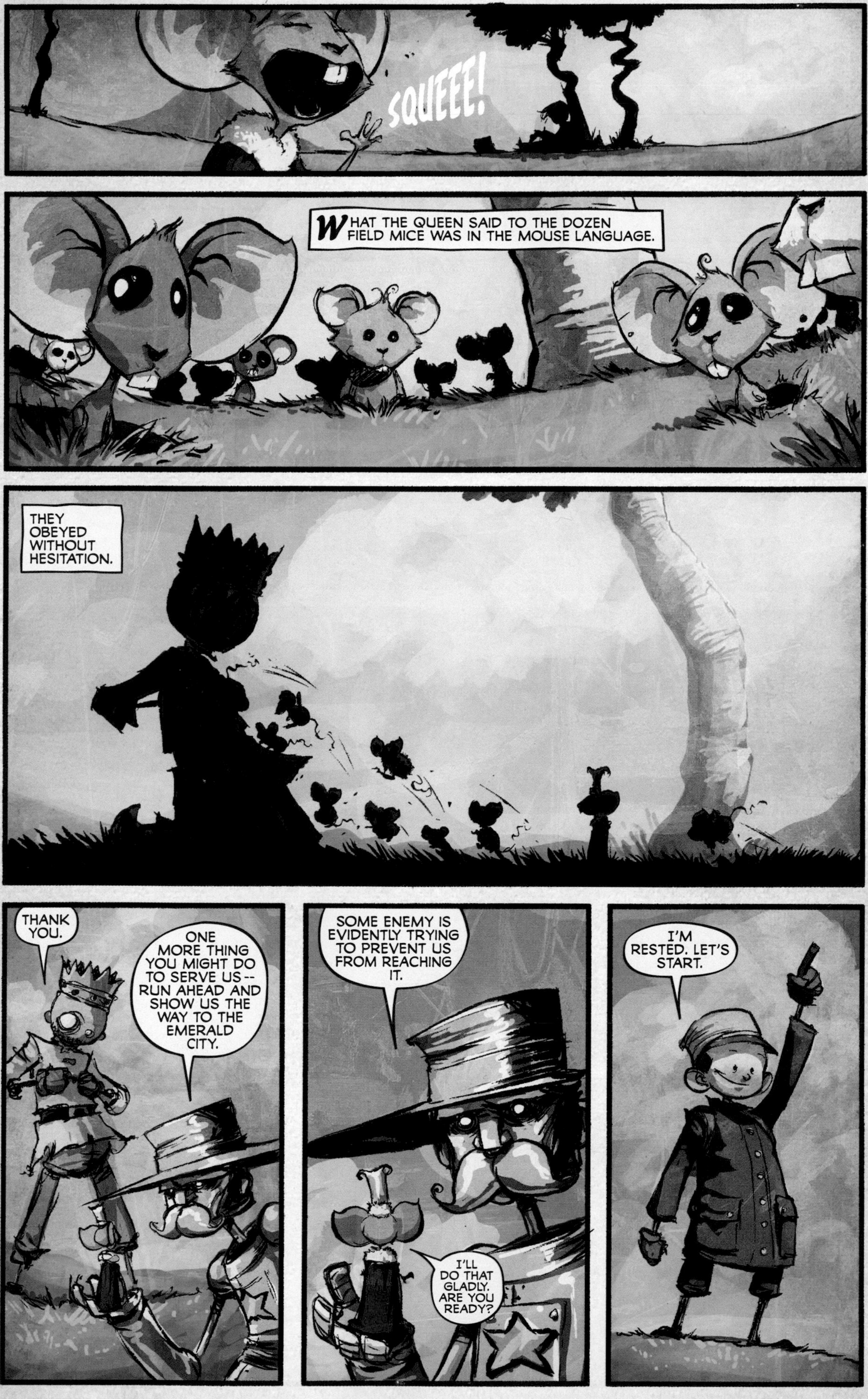
SQUEEE!
WHAT THE QUEEN SAID TO THE DOZEN FIELD MICE WAS IN THE MOUSE LANGUAGE.
THEY OBEYED WITHOUT HESITATION.
THANK YOU.
ONE MORE THING YOU MIGHT DO TO SERVE US-- RUN AHEAD AND SHOW US THE WAY TO THE EMERALD CITY.
SOME ENEMY IS EVIDENTLY TRYING TO PREVENT US FROM REACHING IT.
I'LL DO THAT GLADLY. ARE YOU READY?
I'M RESTED. LET'S START.

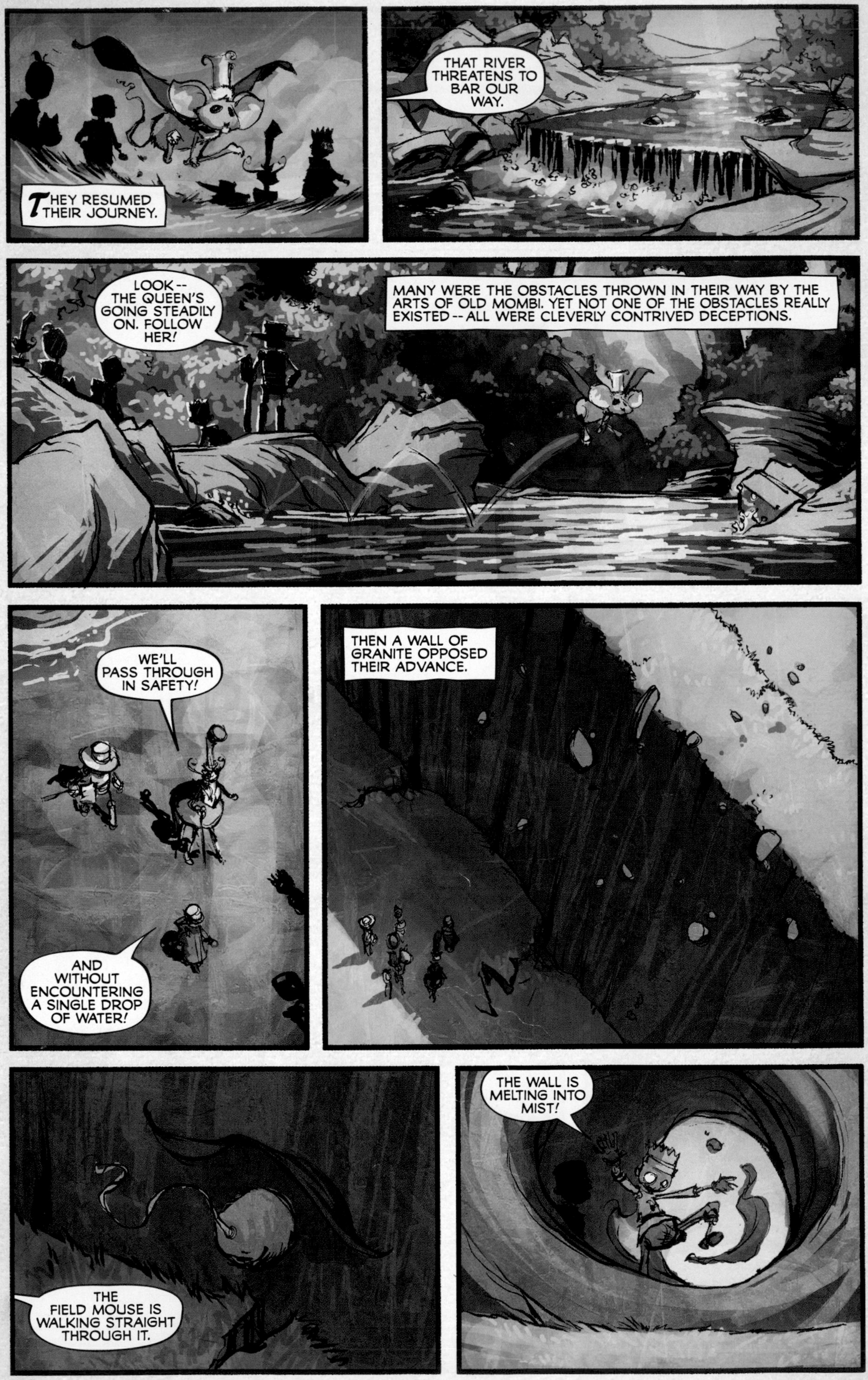
THEY RESUMED THEIR JOURNEY.
THAT RIVER THREATENS TO BAR OUR WAY.
LOOK -- THE QUEEN'S GOING STEADILY ON. FOLLOW HER!
MANY WERE THE OBSTACLES THROWN IN THEIR WAY BY THE ARTS OF OLD MOMBI. YET NOT ONE OF THE OBSTACLES REALLY EXISTED -- ALL WERE CLEVERLY CONTRIVED DECEPTIONS.
WE'LL PASS THROUGH IN SAFETY!
AND WITHOUT ENCOUNTERING A SINGLE DROP OF WATER!
THEN A WALL OF GRANITE OPPOSED THEIR ADVANCE.
THE FIELD MOUSE IS WALKING STRAIGHT THROUGH IT.
THE WALL IS MELTING INTO MIST!

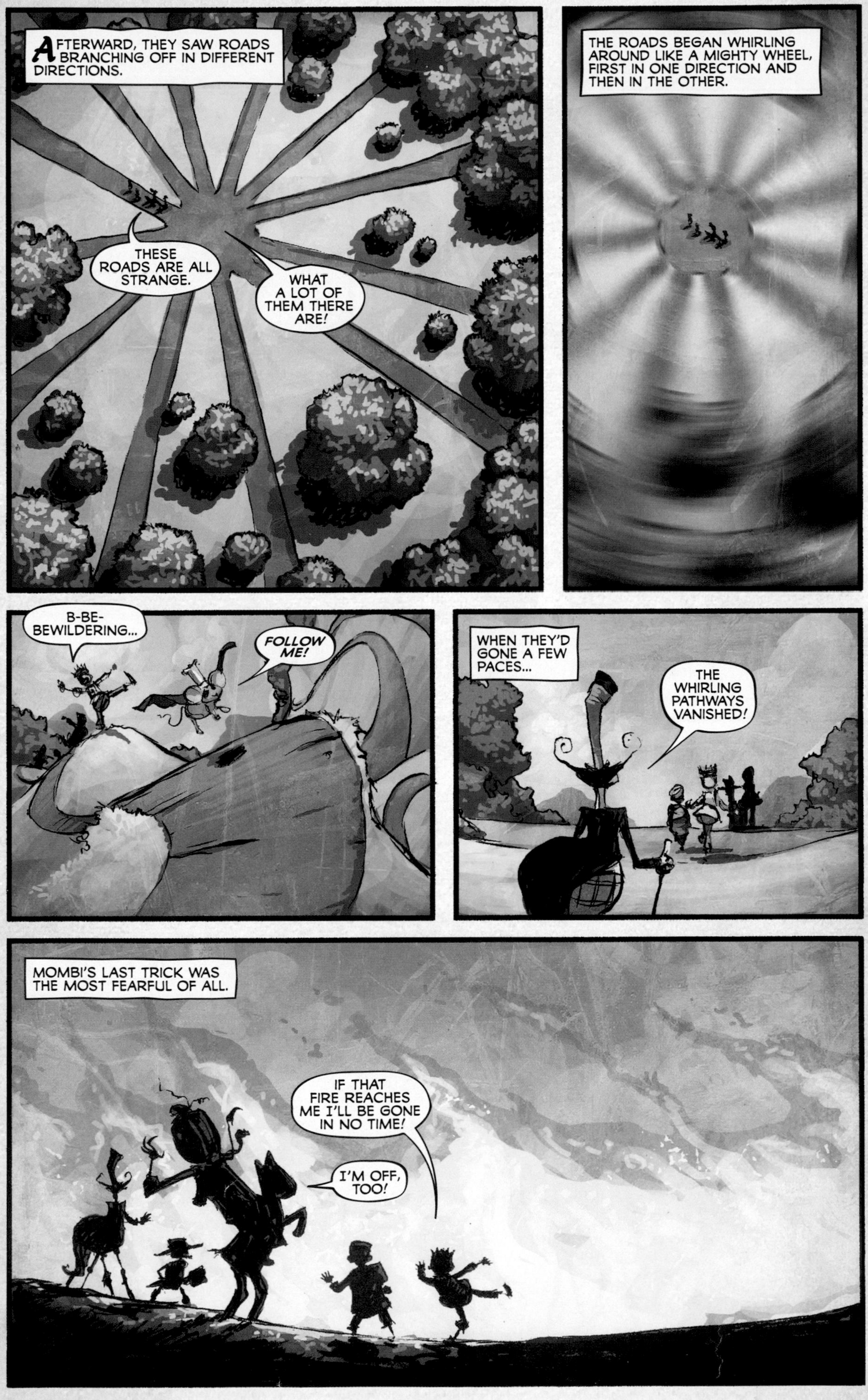
AFTERWARD, THEY SAW ROADS BRANCHING OFF IN DIFFERENT DIRECTIONS.
THESE ROADS ARE ALL STRANGE.
WHAT A LOT OF THEM THERE ARE!
THE ROADS BEGAN WHIRLING AROUND LIKE A MIGHTY WHEEL, FIRST IN ONE DIRECTION AND THEN IN THE OTHER.
B-BE-BEWILDERING...
FOLLOW ME!
WHEN THEY'D GONE A FEW PACES...
THE WHIRLING PATHWAYS VANISHED!
MOMBI'S LAST TRICK WAS THE MOST FEARFUL OF ALL.
IF THAT FIRE REACHES ME I'LL BE GONE IN NO TIME!
I'M OFF, TOO!

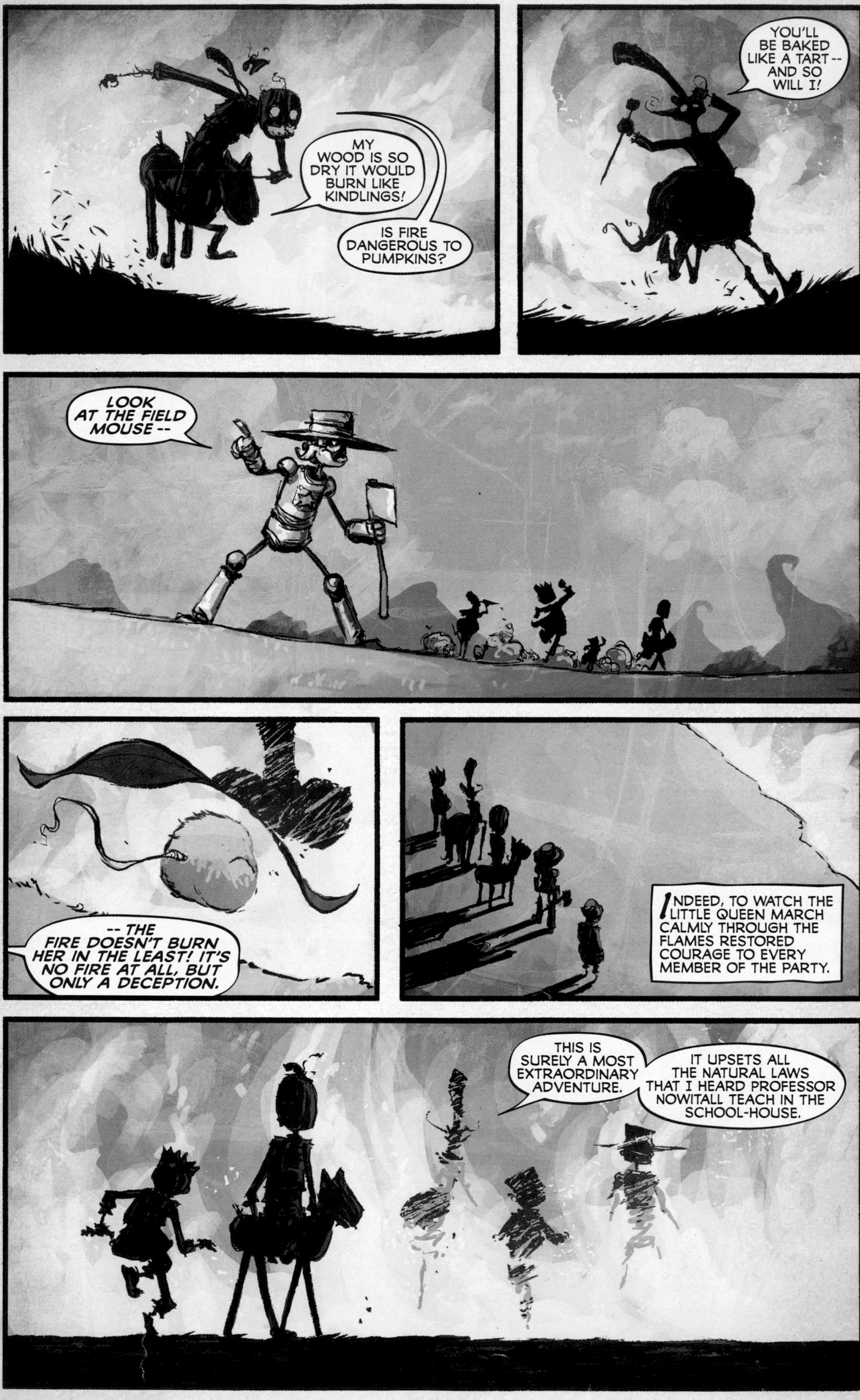
MY WOOD IS SO DRY IT WOULD BURN LIKE KINDLINGS!
IS FIRE DANGEROUS TO PUMPKINS?
YOU'LL BE BAKED LIKE A TART -- AND SO WILL I!
LOOK AT THE FIELD MOUSE --
-- THE FIRE DOESN'T BURN HER IN THE LEAST! IT'S NO FIRE AT ALL, BUT ONLY A DECEPTION.
INDEED, TO WATCH THE LITTLE QUEEN MARCH CALMLY THROUGH THE FLAMES RESTORED COURAGE TO EVERY MEMBER OF THE PARTY.
THIS IS SURELY A MOST EXTRAORDINARY ADVENTURE.
IT UPSETS ALL THE NATURAL LAWS THAT I HEARD PROFESSOR NOWITALL TEACH IN THE SCHOOL-HOUSE.

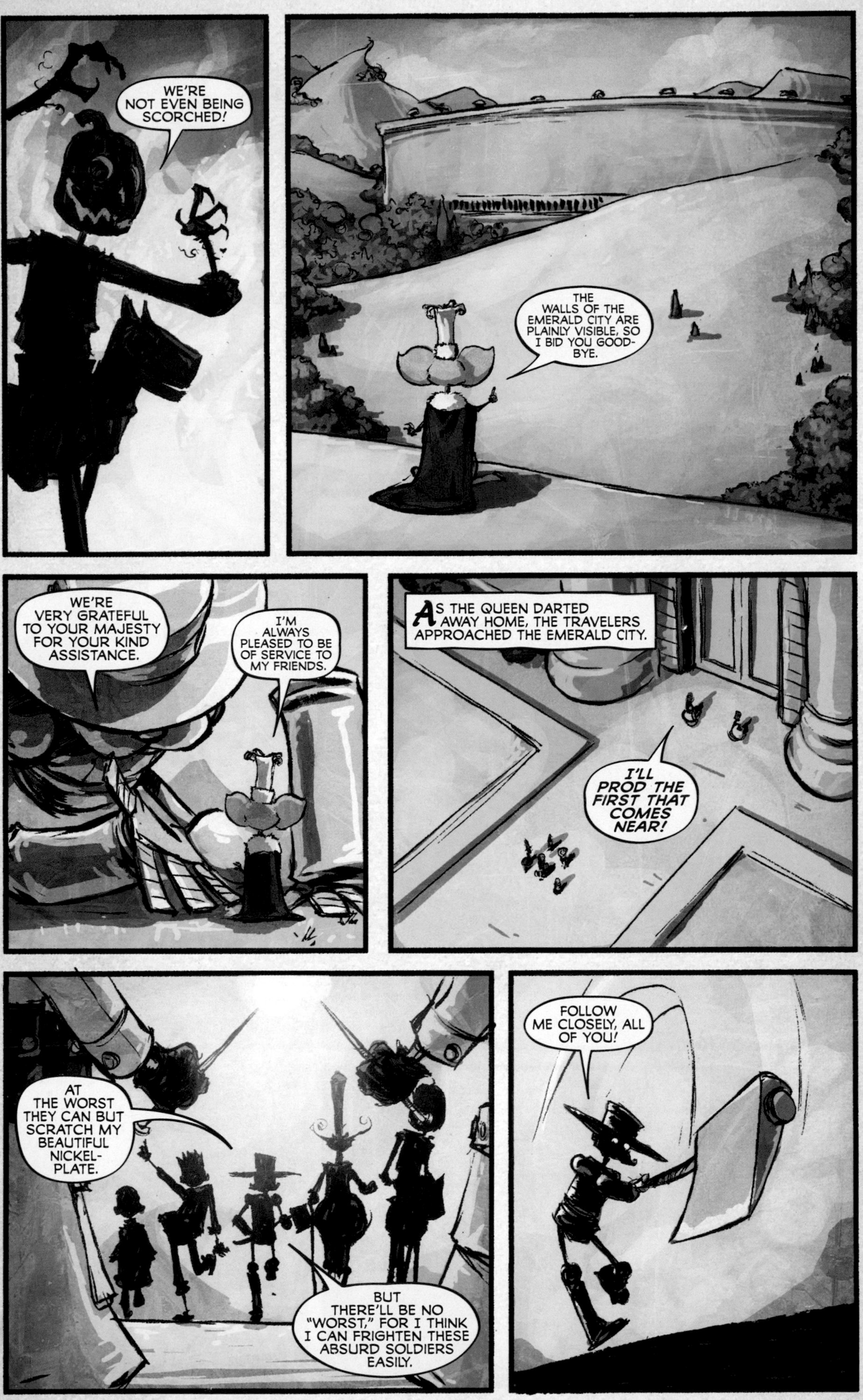

WE'RE NOT EVEN BEING SCORCHED!
THE WALLS OF THE EMERALD CITY ARE PLAINLY VISIBLE, SO I BID YOU GOOD-BYE.
WE'RE VERY GRATEFUL TO YOUR MAJESTY FOR YOUR KIND ASSISTANCE.
I'M ALWAYS PLEASED TO BE OF SERVICE TO MY FRIENDS.
AS THE QUEEN DARTED AWAY HOME, THE TRAVELERS APPROACHED THE EMERALD CITY.
I'LL PROD THE FIRST THAT COMES NEAR!
AT THE WORST THEY CAN BUT SCRATCH MY BEAUTIFUL NICKEL-PLATE.
BUT THERE'LL BE NO "WORST," FOR I THINK I CAN FRIGHTEN THESE ABSURD SOLDIERS EASILY.
FOLLOW ME CLOSELY, ALL OF YOU!

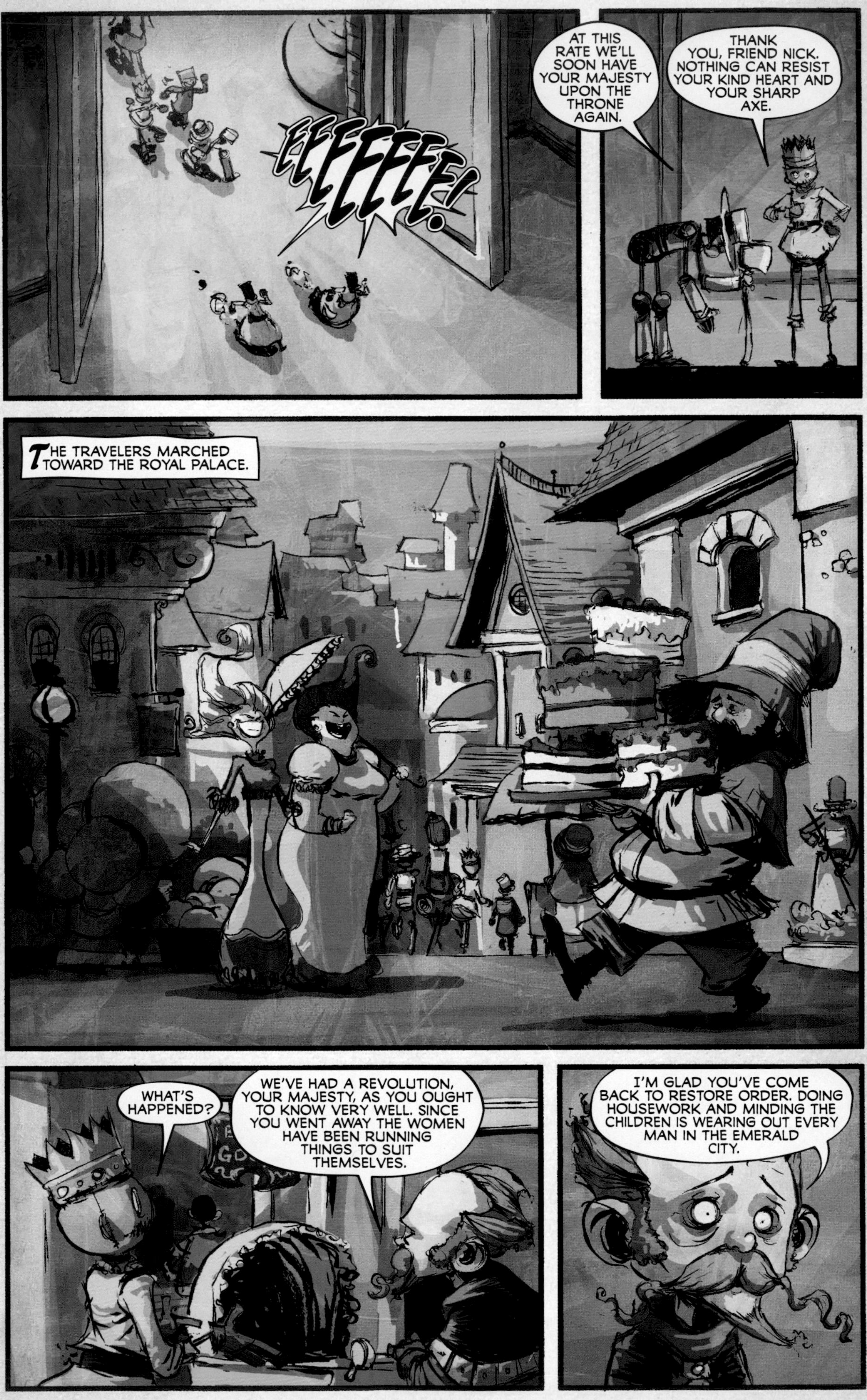
EEEEEEEE!
AT THIS RATE WE'LL SOON HAVE YOUR MAJESTY UPON THE THRONE AGAIN.
THANK YOU, FRIEND NICK. NOTHING CAN RESIST YOUR KIND HEART AND YOUR SHARP AXE.
THE TRAVELERS MARCHED TOWARD THE ROYAL PALACE.
WHAT'S HAPPENED?
WE'VE HAD A REVOLUTION, YOUR MAJESTY, AS YOU OUGHT TO KNOW VERY WELL. SINCE YOU WENT AWAY THE WOMEN HAVE BEEN RUNNING THINGS TO SUIT THEMSELVES.
I'M GLAD YOU'VE COME BACK TO RESTORE ORDER. DOING HOUSEWORK AND MINDING THE CHILDREN IS WEARING OUT EVERY MAN IN THE EMERALD CITY.

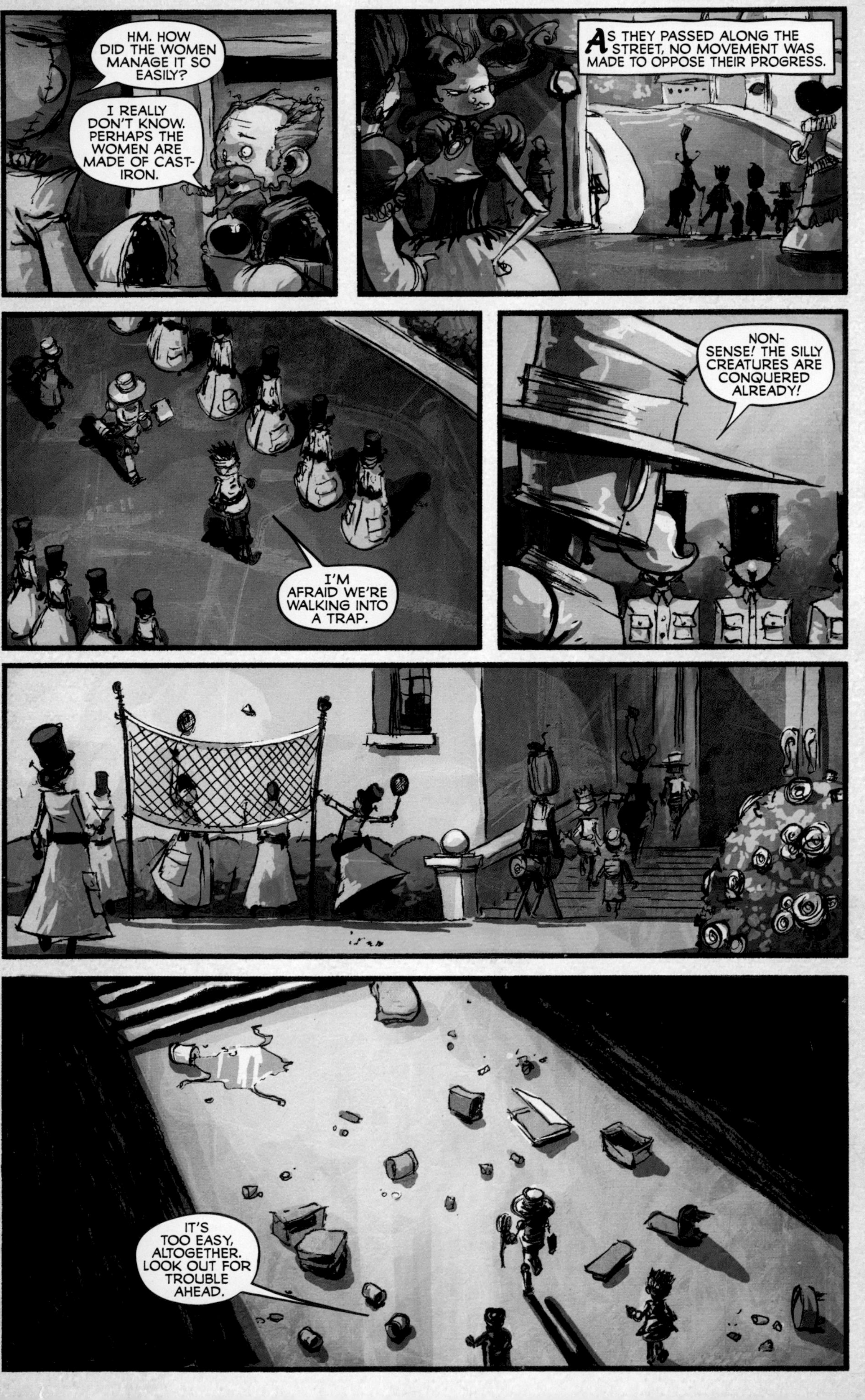
HM. HOW DID THE WOMEN MANAGE IT SO EASILY?
I REALLY DON'T KNOW. PERHAPS THE WOMEN ARE MADE OF CAST-IRON.
AS THEY PASSED ALONG THE STREET, NO MOVEMENT WAS MADE TO OPPOSE THEIR PROGRESS.
I'M AFRAID WE'RE WALKING INTO A TRAP.
NON-SENSE! THE SILLY CREATURES ARE CONQUERED ALREADY!
IT'S TOO EASY, ALTOGETHER. LOOK OUT FOR TROUBLE AHEAD.

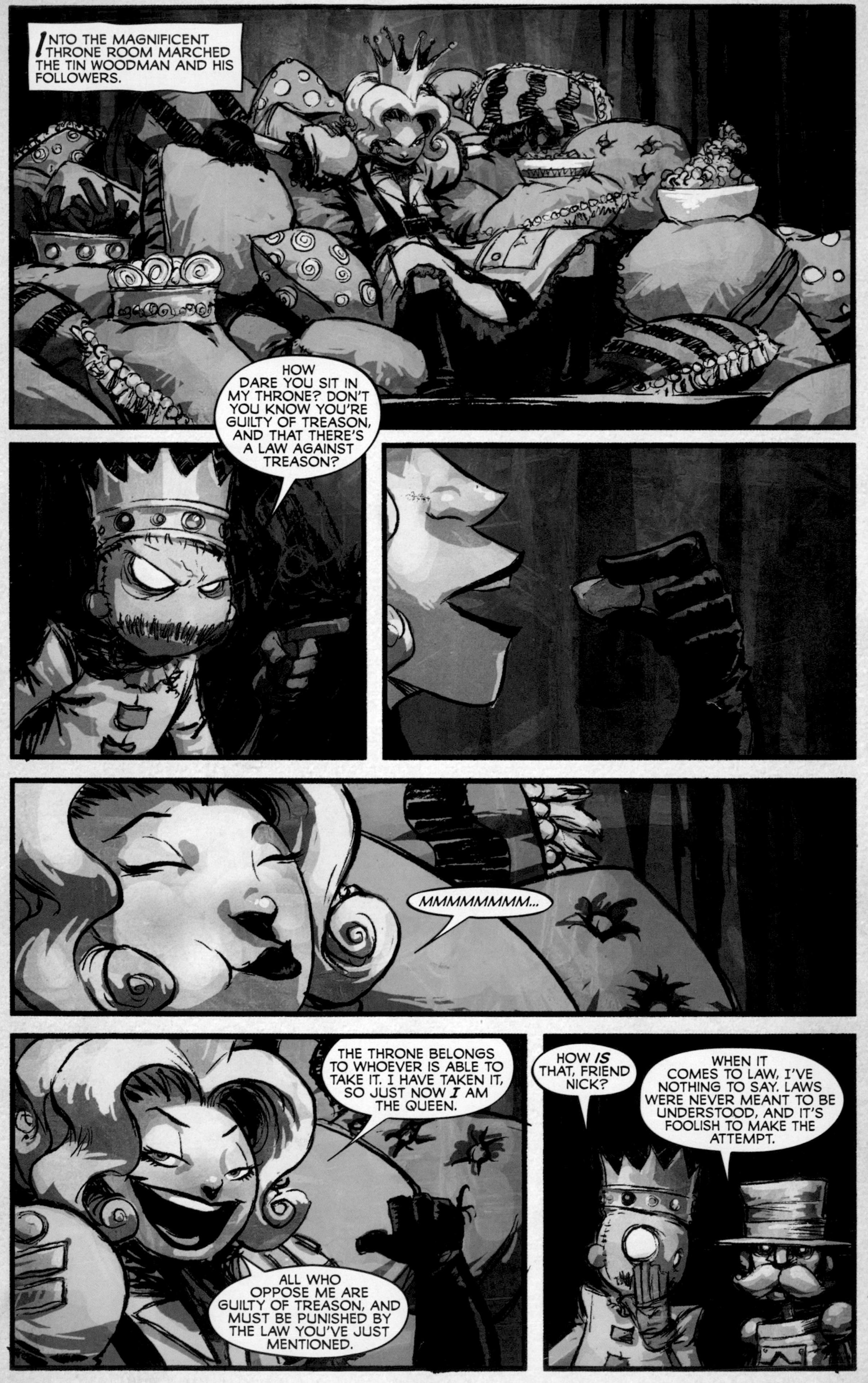
INTO THE MAGNIFICENT THRONE ROOM MARCHED THE TIN WOODMAN AND HIS FOLLOWERS.
HOW DARE YOU SIT IN MY THRONE? DON'T YOU KNOW YOU'RE GUILTY OF TREASON, AND THAT THERE'S A LAW AGAINST TREASON?
MMMMMMMMM...
THE THRONE BELONGS TO WHOEVER IS ABLE TO TAKE IT. I HAVE TAKEN IT, SO JUST NOW I AM THE QUEEN.
ALL WHO OPPOSE ME ARE GUILTY OF TREASON, AND MUST BE PUNISHED BY THE LAW YOU'VE JUST MENTIONED.
HOW IS THAT, FRIEND NICK?
WHEN IT COMES TO LAW, I'VE NOTHING TO SAY. LAWS WERE NEVER MEANT TO BE UNDERSTOOD, AND IT'S FOOLISH TO MAKE THE ATTEMPT.

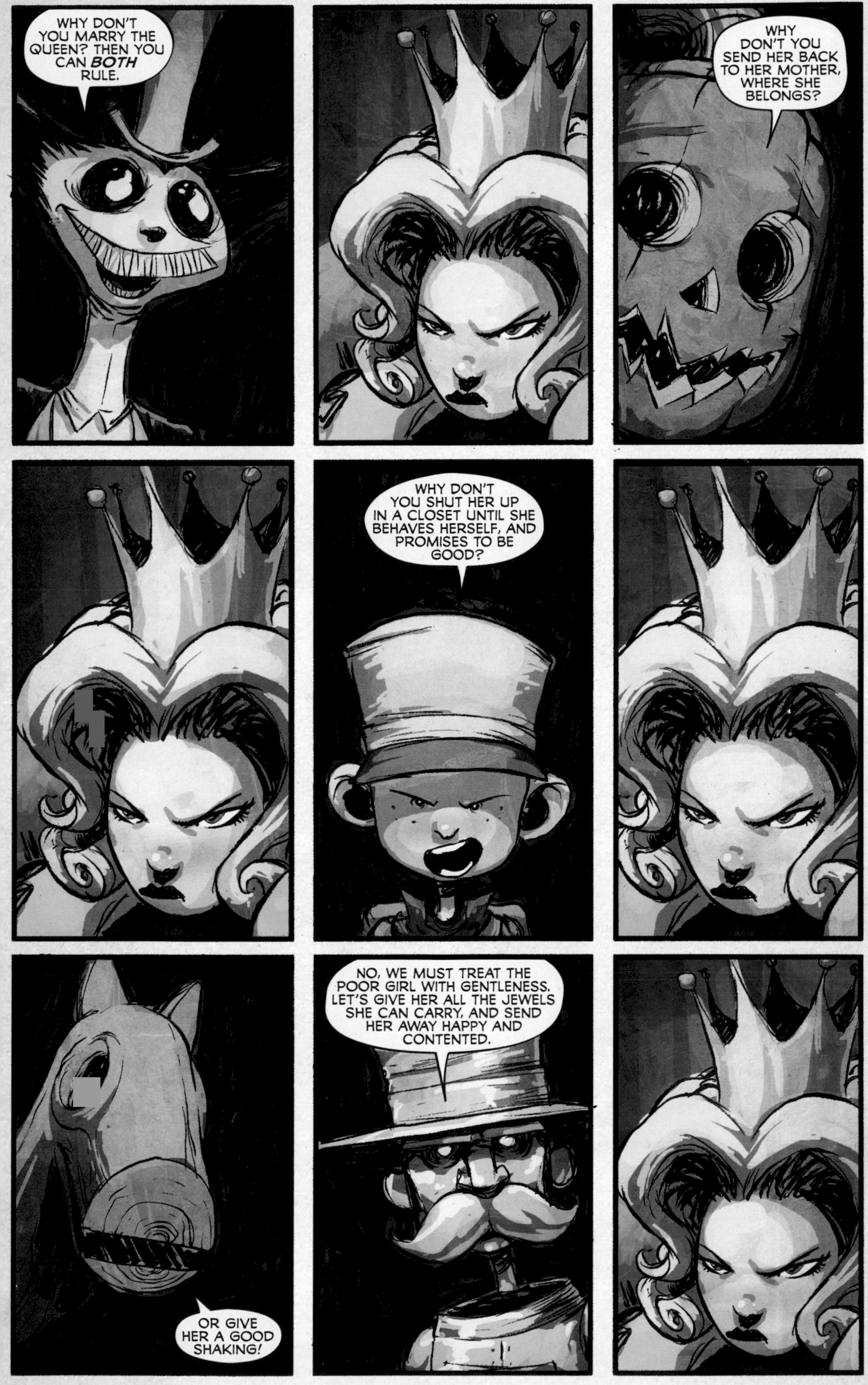
WHY DON'T YOU MARRY THE QUEEN? THEN YOU CAN *BOTH* RULE.
WHY DON'T YOU SEND HER BACK TO HER MOTHER, WHERE SHE BELONGS?
WHY DON'T YOU SHUT HER UP IN A CLOSET UNTIL SHE BEHAVES HERSELF, AND PROMISES TO BE GOOD?
OR GIVE HER A GOOD SHAKING!
NO, WE MUST TREAT THE POOR GIRL WITH GENTLENESS. LET'S GIVE HER ALL THE JEWELS SHE CAN CARRY, AND SEND HER AWAY HAPPY AND CONTENTED.

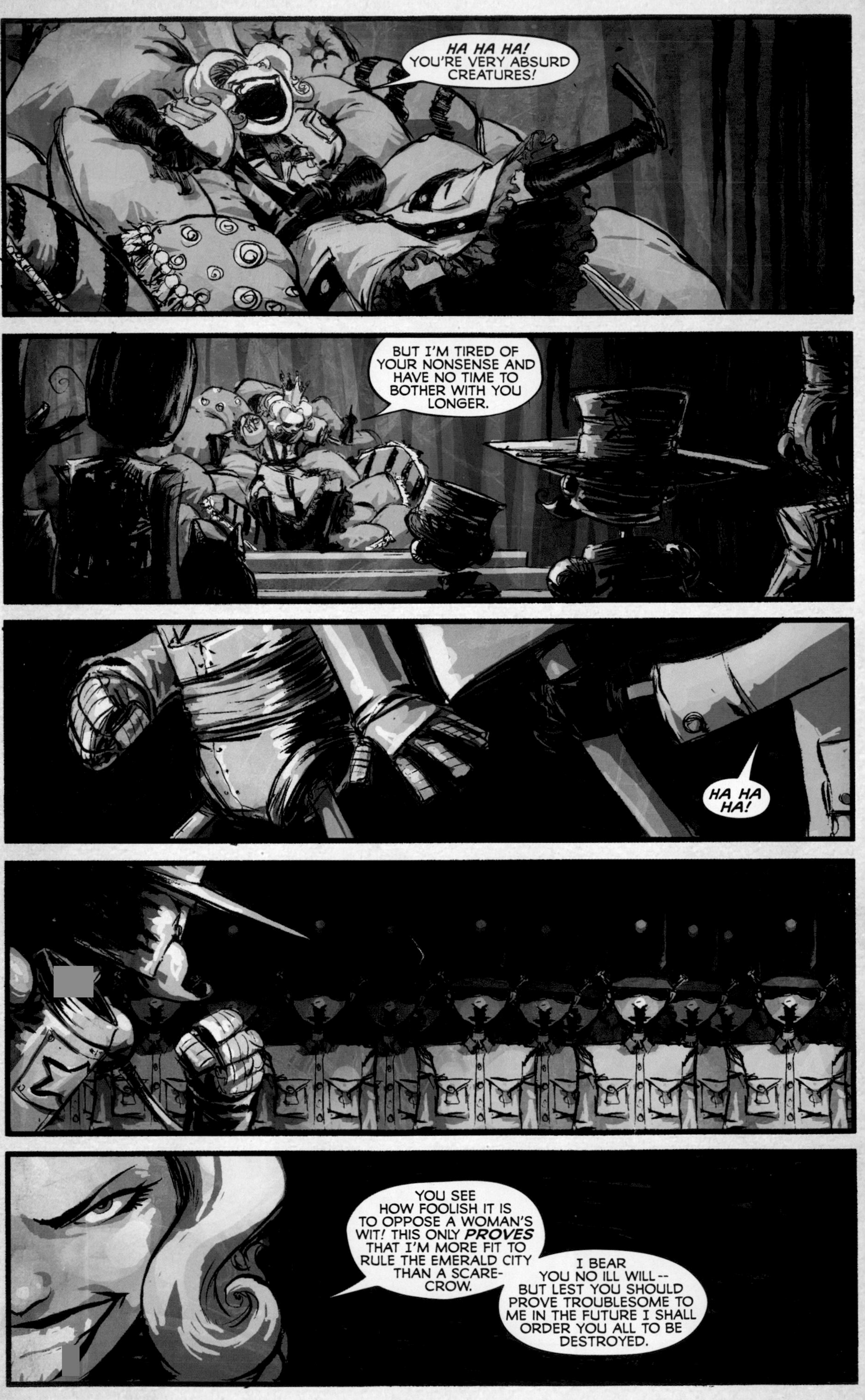
HA HA HA! YOU'RE VERY ABSURD CREATURES!
BUT I'M TIRED OF YOUR NONSENSE AND HAVE NO TIME TO BOTHER WITH YOU LONGER.
HA HA HA!
YOU SEE HOW FOOLISH IT IS TO OPPOSE A WOMAN'S WIT! THIS ONLY PROVES THAT I'M MORE FIT TO RULE THE EMERALD CITY THAN A SCARE-CROW.
I BEAR YOU NO ILL WILL -- BUT LEST YOU SHOULD PROVE TROUBLESOME TO ME IN THE FUTURE I SHALL ORDER YOU ALL TO BE DESTROYED.

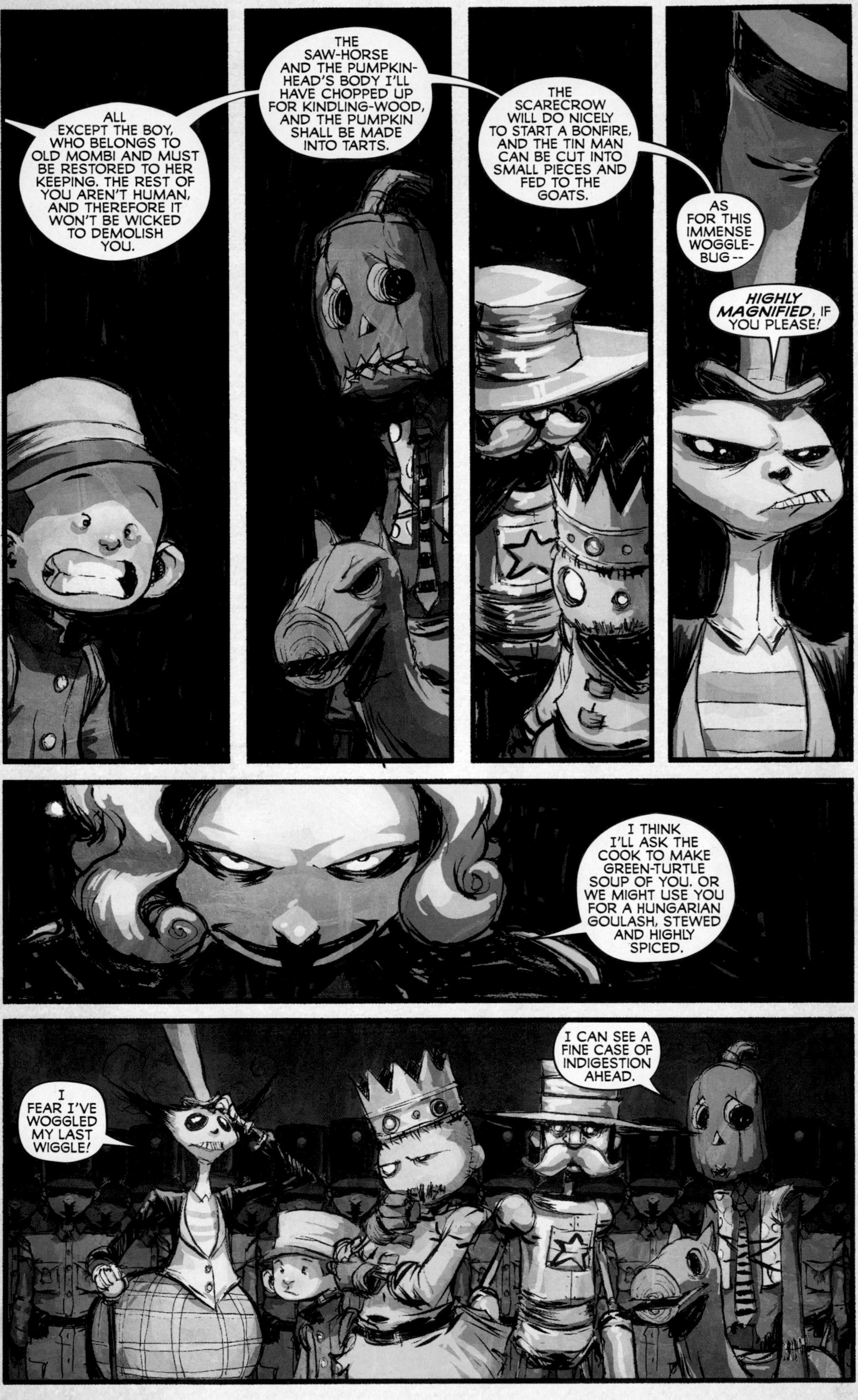
ALL EXCEPT THE BOY, WHO BELONGS TO OLD MOMBI AND MUST BE RESTORED TO HER KEEPING. THE REST OF YOU AREN'T HUMAN, AND THEREFORE IT WON'T BE WICKED TO DEMOLISH YOU.
THE SAW-HORSE AND THE PUMPKIN-HEAD'S BODY I'LL HAVE CHOPPED UP FOR KINDLING-WOOD, AND THE PUMPKIN SHALL BE MADE INTO TARTS.
THE SCARECROW WILL DO NICELY TO START A BONFIRE, AND THE TIN MAN CAN BE CUT INTO SMALL PIECES AND FED TO THE GOATS.
AS FOR THIS IMMENSE WOGGLE-BUG --
HIGHLY MAGNIFIED, IF YOU PLEASE!
I THINK I'LL ASK THE COOK TO MAKE GREEN-TURTLE SOUP OF YOU. OR WE MIGHT USE YOU FOR A HUNGARIAN GOULASH, STEWED AND HIGHLY SPICED.
I FEAR I'VE WOGGLED MY LAST WIGGLE!
I CAN SEE A FINE CASE OF INDIGESTION AHEAD.

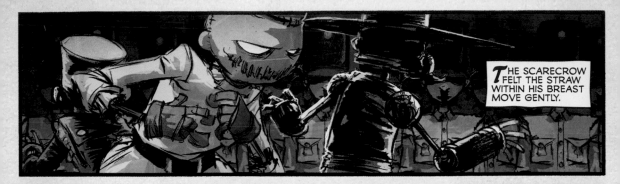

THE SCARECROW FELT THE STRAW WITHIN HIS BREAST MOVE GENTLY.

EEEEEEEK!

EEEEEEEEE!

EEEEEEE!

EEEEEEE!

YOWWWWWWWWW...

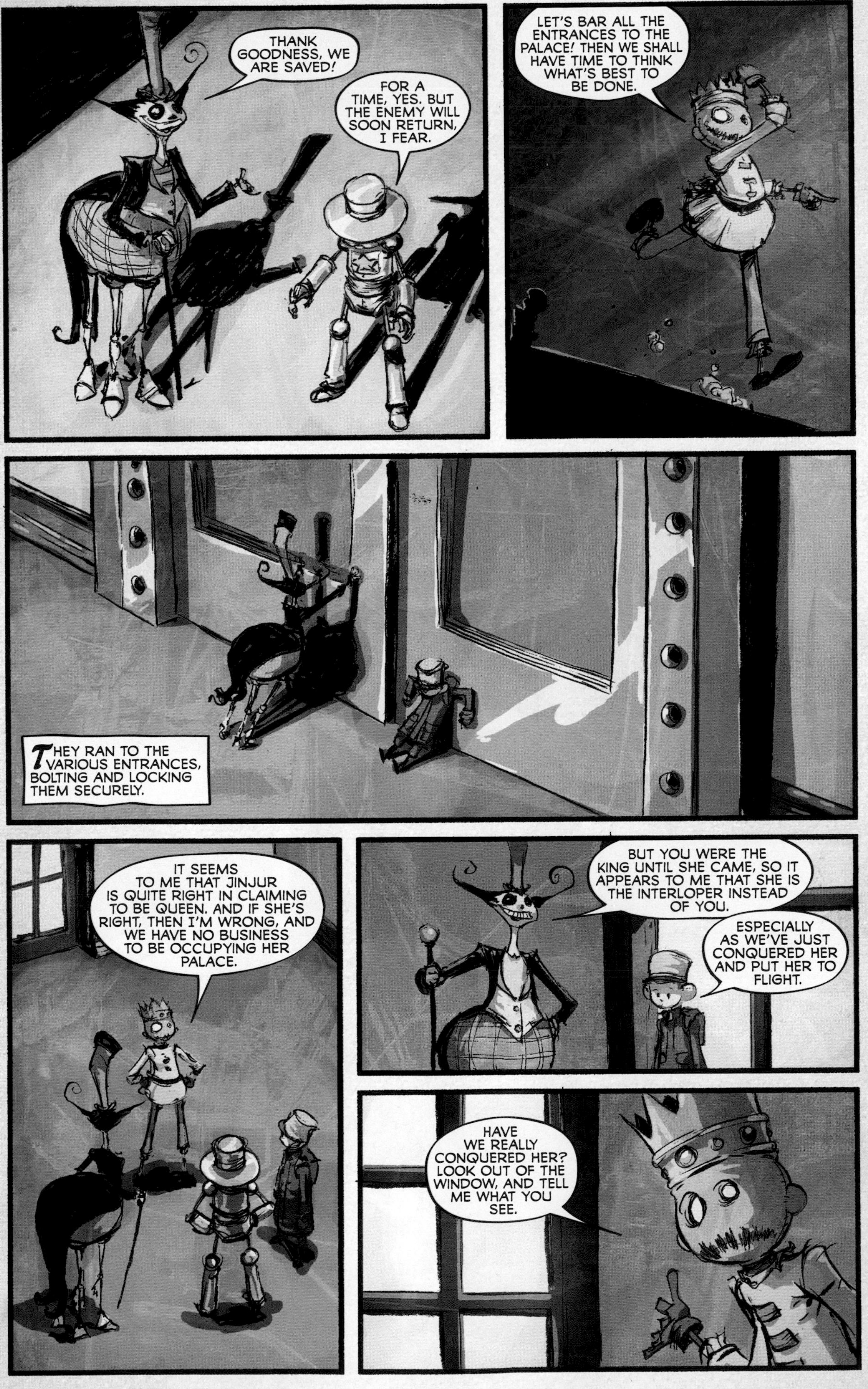
THANK GOODNESS, WE ARE SAVED!
FOR A TIME, YES. BUT THE ENEMY WILL SOON RETURN, I FEAR.
LET'S BAR ALL THE ENTRANCES TO THE PALACE! THEN WE SHALL HAVE TIME TO THINK WHAT'S BEST TO BE DONE.
THEY RAN TO THE VARIOUS ENTRANCES, BOLTING AND LOCKING THEM SECURELY.
IT SEEMS TO ME THAT JINJUR IS QUITE RIGHT IN CLAIMING TO BE QUEEN. AND IF SHE'S RIGHT, THEN I'M WRONG, AND WE HAVE NO BUSINESS TO BE OCCUPYING HER PALACE.
BUT YOU WERE THE KING UNTIL SHE CAME, SO IT APPEARS TO ME THAT SHE IS THE INTERLOPER INSTEAD OF YOU.
ESPECIALLY AS WE'VE JUST CONQUERED HER AND PUT HER TO FLIGHT.
HAVE WE REALLY CONQUERED HER? LOOK OUT OF THE WINDOW, AND TELL ME WHAT YOU SEE.

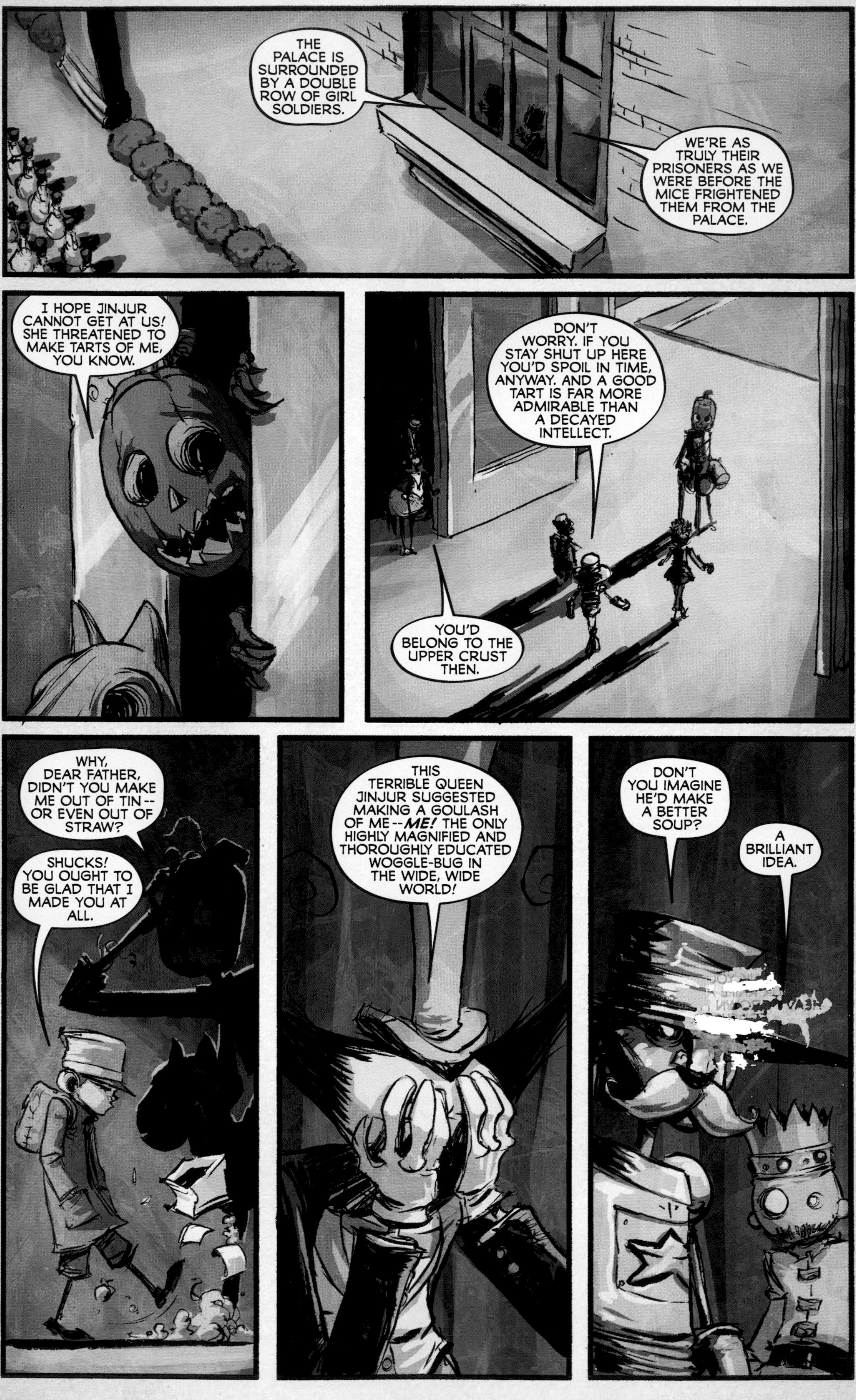
THE PALACE IS SURROUNDED BY A DOUBLE ROW OF GIRL SOLDIERS.
WE'RE AS TRULY THEIR PRISONERS AS WE WERE BEFORE THE MICE FRIGHTENED THEM FROM THE PALACE.
I HOPE JINJUR CANNOT GET AT US! SHE THREATENED TO MAKE TARTS OF ME, YOU KNOW.
DON'T WORRY. IF YOU STAY SHUT UP HERE YOU'D SPOIL IN TIME, ANYWAY. AND A GOOD TART IS FAR MORE ADMIRABLE THAN A DECAYED INTELLECT.
YOU'D BELONG TO THE UPPER CRUST THEN.
WHY, DEAR FATHER, DIDN'T YOU MAKE ME OUT OF TIN--OR EVEN OUT OF STRAW?
SHUCKS! YOU OUGHT TO BE GLAD THAT I MADE YOU AT ALL.
THIS TERRIBLE QUEEN JINJUR SUGGESTED MAKING A GOULASH OF ME--*ME!* THE ONLY HIGHLY MAGNIFIED AND THOROUGHLY EDUCATED WOGGLE-BUG IN THE WIDE, WIDE WORLD!
DON'T YOU IMAGINE HE'D MAKE A BETTER SOUP?
A BRILLIANT IDEA.

I CAN SEE, IN MY MIND'S EYE, THE GOATS EATING SMALL PIECES OF MY DEAR COMRADE, THE TIN WOOD-MAN...

...WHILE MY SOUP IS BEING COOKED ON A BONFIRE BUILT OF THE SAW-HORSE AND JACK PUMPKINHEAD'S BODY...

...AND QUEEN JINJUR WATCHES ME BOIL WHILE SHE FEEDS THE FLAMES WITH MY FRIEND THE SCARECROW!

IT CAN'T HAPPEN FOR SOME TIME, FOR WE SHALL BE ABLE TO KEEP JINJUR OUT OF THE PALACE UNTIL SHE MANAGES TO BREAK DOWN THE DOORS.

IN THE MEANTIME I'M LIABLE TO STARVE TO DEATH.

I THINK THAT I COULD LIVE FOR SOME TIME ON JACK PUMPKIN-HEAD. NOT THAT I PREFER PUMPKINS FOR FOOD --

HOW *HEARTLESS!*

LET'S END THIS MOURNFUL TALK AND TRY TO DISCOVER A MEANS TO ESCAPE.

I BELIEVE I'LL THINK FOR A FEW MINUTES, SO I'LL THANK YOU, TIP, TO GET OUT YO... AND RIP THIS HEAVY CROWN FROM MY FOREHEAD.

OOPS!

WHAT'S THIS?

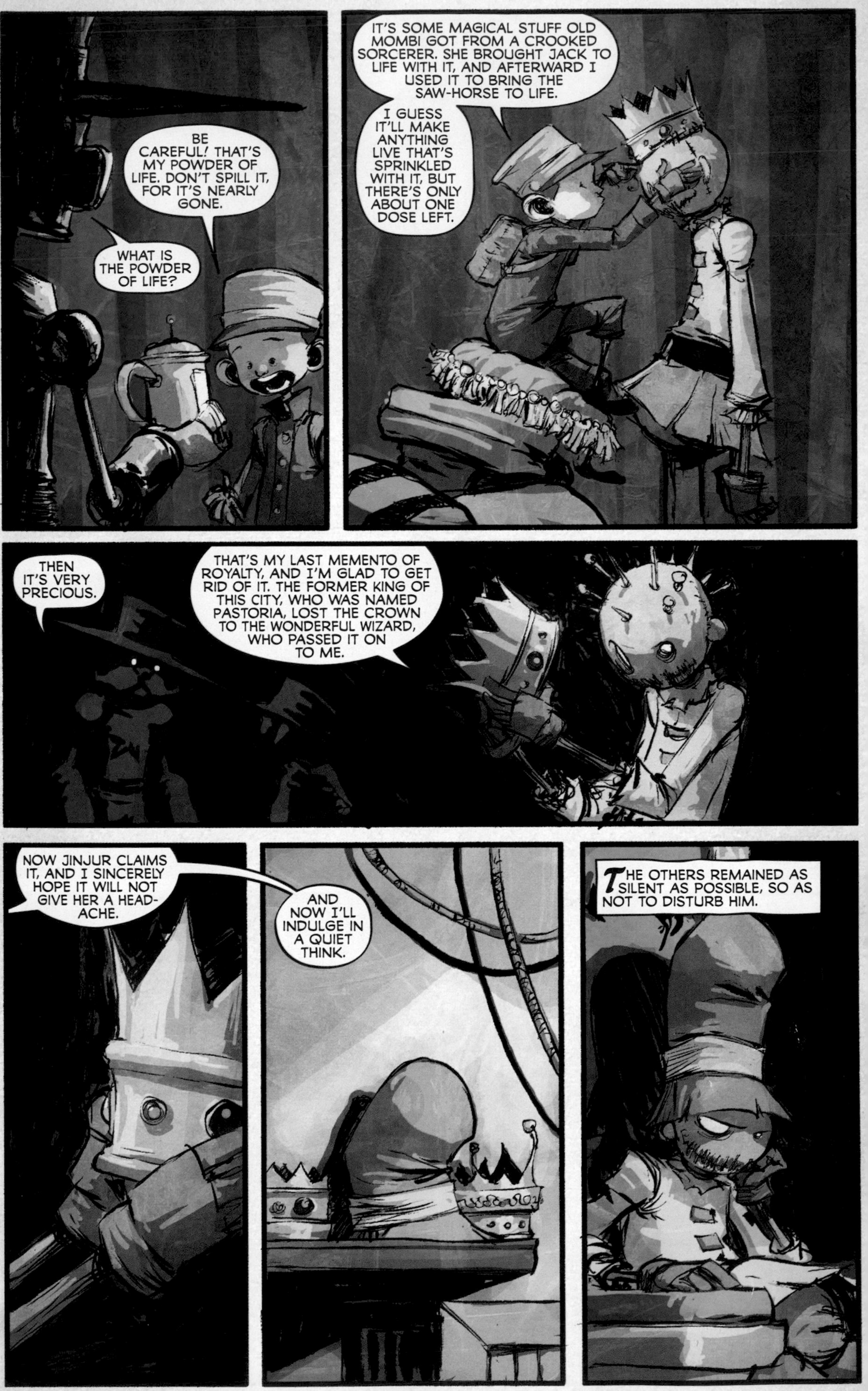
BE CAREFUL! THAT'S MY POWDER OF LIFE. DON'T SPILL IT, FOR IT'S NEARLY GONE.
WHAT IS THE POWDER OF LIFE?
IT'S SOME MAGICAL STUFF OLD MOMBI GOT FROM A CROOKED SORCERER. SHE BROUGHT JACK TO LIFE WITH IT, AND AFTERWARD I USED IT TO BRING THE SAW-HORSE TO LIFE.
I GUESS IT'LL MAKE ANYTHING LIVE THAT'S SPRINKLED WITH IT, BUT THERE'S ONLY ABOUT ONE DOSE LEFT.
THEN IT'S VERY PRECIOUS.
THAT'S MY LAST MEMENTO OF ROYALTY, AND I'M GLAD TO GET RID OF IT. THE FORMER KING OF THIS CITY, WHO WAS NAMED PASTORIA, LOST THE CROWN TO THE WONDERFUL WIZARD, WHO PASSED IT ON TO ME.
NOW JINJUR CLAIMS IT, AND I SINCERELY HOPE IT WILL NOT GIVE HER A HEAD-ACHE.
AND NOW I'LL INDULGE IN A QUIET THINK.
THE OTHERS REMAINED AS SILENT AS POSSIBLE, SO AS NOT TO DISTURB HIM.

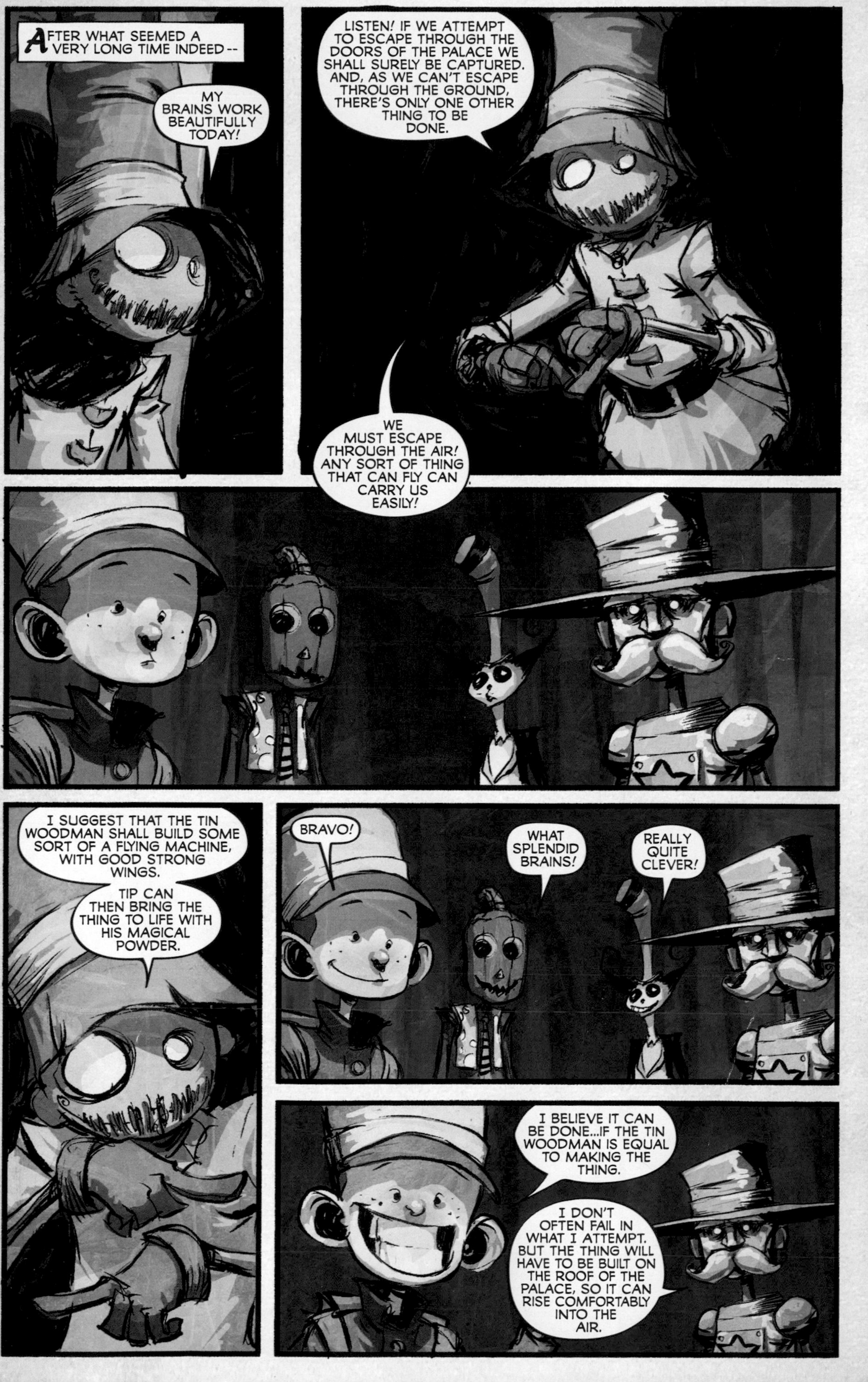

AFTER WHAT SEEMED A VERY LONG TIME INDEED--
MY BRAINS WORK BEAUTIFULLY TODAY!
LISTEN! IF WE ATTEMPT TO ESCAPE THROUGH THE DOORS OF THE PALACE WE SHALL SURELY BE CAPTURED. AND, AS WE CAN'T ESCAPE THROUGH THE GROUND, THERE'S ONLY ONE OTHER THING TO BE DONE.
WE MUST ESCAPE THROUGH THE AIR! ANY SORT OF THING THAT CAN FLY CAN CARRY US EASILY!
I SUGGEST THAT THE TIN WOODMAN SHALL BUILD SOME SORT OF A FLYING MACHINE, WITH GOOD STRONG WINGS.
TIP CAN THEN BRING THE THING TO LIFE WITH HIS MAGICAL POWDER.
BRAVO!
WHAT SPLENDID BRAINS!
REALLY QUITE CLEVER!
I BELIEVE IT CAN BE DONE...IF THE TIN WOODMAN IS EQUAL TO MAKING THE THING.
I DON'T OFTEN FAIL IN WHAT I ATTEMPT. BUT THE THING WILL HAVE TO BE BUILT ON THE ROOF OF THE PALACE, SO IT CAN RISE COMFORTABLY INTO THE AIR.

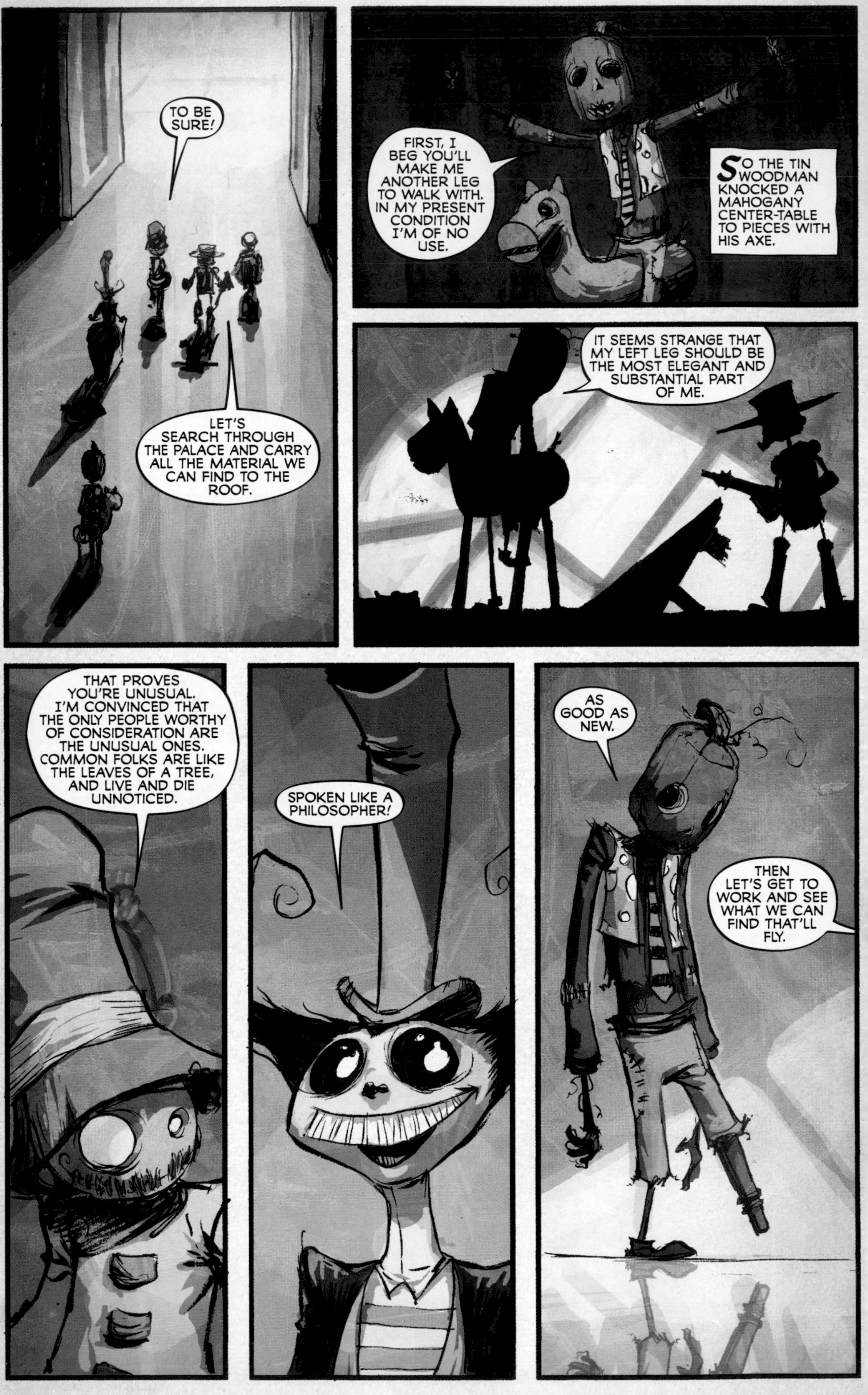
TO BE SURE!
LET'S SEARCH THROUGH THE PALACE AND CARRY ALL THE MATERIAL WE CAN FIND TO THE ROOF.
FIRST, I BEG YOU'LL MAKE ME ANOTHER LEG TO WALK WITH. IN MY PRESENT CONDITION I'M OF NO USE.
SO THE TIN WOODMAN KNOCKED A MAHOGANY CENTER-TABLE TO PIECES WITH HIS AXE.
IT SEEMS STRANGE THAT MY LEFT LEG SHOULD BE THE MOST ELEGANT AND SUBSTANTIAL PART OF ME.
THAT PROVES YOU'RE UNUSUAL. I'M CONVINCED THAT THE ONLY PEOPLE WORTHY OF CONSIDERATION ARE THE UNUSUAL ONES. COMMON FOLKS ARE LIKE THE LEAVES OF A TREE, AND LIVE AND DIE UNNOTICED.
SPOKEN LIKE A PHILOSOPHER!
AS GOOD AS NEW.
THEN LET'S GET TO WORK AND SEE WHAT WE CAN FIND THAT'LL FLY.